Flashbacks Of Flashforwards

Speculative Stories

W. J. Manares

Ukiyoto Publishing

All global publishing rights are held by

Ukiyoto Publishing

Published in 2023

ISBN 9789360167370

This is a work of fiction. Names, characters, businesses, places, events, locales, and incidents are either the products of the author's imagination or used in a fictitious manner. Any resemblance to actual persons, living or dead, or actual events is purely coincidental.

www.ukiyoto.com

To Anne McCaffrey, the "Mother of Speculative Fiction", on her birthday (in Pern)

Contents

Fotorat

The fat Sundog named Fotorat was looking for a special ascendant, no other than her father.

She's at the halfway mark of her life and still living as a bastard. Fotorat was staying with her friends at a pet facility until yesterday when a sunquake occured. Its goosebumping shakes damaged the cage where she was locked up for the last 20 years.

Fotorat was found alone wandering on the streets of Sinus. She has no worries now, nothing to be afraid of. Fotorat got a strong and flaring body due to her almost 9 years work out and intensive training.

She was only 6 when her father left them to join the army of Beeshano that fights for their rights as legitimate Sundogs.

Today, it's almost impossible to find him. She finished touring all of the pavements and alleys visible to the canine eye but she failed.

Early morning the next day, Fotorat was awakened by the voices around her. A pack of male Sundogs are looking for a mate. Sounds good!

Brao

Another boring day! Brao hugged his bag while he jogged inside the enchanted oval of Core Park.

Catroots and Peekpack-eaters were hovering this area. They're victimizing rampantly and randomly.

You must walk away in a jiffy before they did the art of shape-shifting. Into terrifying hogs with warts like quartz. Actually, they're aliens from the former moon, Ae. They squatted on Margadon Island before establishing their camp here at Core Park through an illegal contract with the Manogres.

You can't trust anyone nowadays. Thanks to the early-warning device attached in the brow of Brao. It's brown for he's a member of the Brownies clan.

Brao actually wanted a black one but it's impossible. Anyone from their clan could be in danger of being captured or the worst, be killed on the spot, if they'll try to switch brown into other tints or change its color by dyeing. "To dye is to die today" was a well-known saying among the Brownies.

Well, the Catroots and Peekpack-eaters has devices in their right brows too. It's either red or orange.

Did I tell you before that all creatures in Core Park have the facial features of a pig?

Rebosa

Rebosa was sad. She was scolded by her mother because of her uncontrollable naughty deeds. She shot a Whalerus dead thinking that the creature was harmful. Rebosa's family paid the blood money for her temporary freedom.

The residents of Fifty Sixth Deep, the ocean where they lived, were disturbed by her repulsive action. Rebosa was sorry. Her eleventacles were sore and her eyes too. They're drowning in tears that wetted the tares and tore down the wheat as they dropped regrets on the bottom of the trench. There grew Acaba weeds that entangled both the microbes and the macrobes. Another crime in the water formations of Stripes, cited in the Amendment.

Rebosa's brothers tried hard to prevent her from feeling down again. They're doing clownish things just to make her laugh all the day long.

Successful indeed, tears of joy overflowed. Rebosa laughed and laughed until the whole area crumbled. The platform where they're located collapsed, and killed all the protesters below. T'was an instant tear-jerker!

Drink-N-Cracker

Goblinorcs and Manogres were playing some card games when a band of Chupacagnomes reached the Subdubpub at Golden Caverns. They're sweaty, tired from the journey behind them.

A hundred mugs of Silbeers and some Sheepchips were cheap enough for their Headlooter to buy. He told his assistant to purchase those special treats for them to consume in order to regain their wit and strength.

Actually, there's nothing special about a Silbeer and a Sheepchip. These treats were so common for the residents of Golden Caverns.

I would love to recommend these "real deals" when you visit our county, south of Mythopia. Here below, please find, the list of our most special "drink-n-cracker" combos:

1. Echavodka and Krakenscapes

2. Herdrhum and Slimmergrunts

3. Burphic and Snorecatchers

4. Dullwizkey and Knobgrubs

5. Cognactus and Shruboots

Happy to serve you.

Khork Of Alup

So this is Lusa, a red asteroid with 4 volcanoes, situated 666 darkyears away from the Neongreen stars of the constellation Gemini. This distant habitat was feared by its neighbors in the Asteroid Lace where it belonged. Only the brave and mighty Srams of Mars built a colony here.

I am the only cold-blooded creature in their fearsome reddish place. I'm Khork the Con from the blue asteroid Alup, where herbivore humanoids lived for the past century after the Bulge Boom event that shaped the entire Omniverse.

I was left alone by my gang. They all died when we landed here, right on the crater of Lusa's most active volcano. Our space vehicle, SV-012 didn't intercept its impending eruption that's why we encountered that tragic loss.

I must survive. I must make Alup proud, if granted to be able to return, to that blue asteroid of ours.

While I'm in solitary moments, I taught myself how to speak, write, and read their peculiar language, Lusi. And I've formulated a plan to conquer Lusa. So that,

I'll become their supreme leader. But first, I need to get out of this Freezone cell.

Human

The game will begin soon. But Zkranch the Manogre and his team were not sure if they could register. The whole Orgeville community will once again participate in a Xannual Bone Smashing Contest.

Zkranch's teammate, Zkritch, found out that the five of them needs a human in order to be qualified in the registration. That is the first requirement.

The second requirement was to bring a tool, a special one, for the smashing game.

The third requirement for each member was a Tickglass, which will be used to know how fast could a contestant pulvurize the poor creature he/she will bring.

And the last requirement was a phoenix's feather for writing the competitor's name on the player's list.

The saddest part for Zkranch's group was the opportunity they will surely miss. Because the first requirement was so hard to find nowadays.

Hermap and the Deworming

The twin suns' ultralavender rays woke Hermap up with an aching brainpan. He got a bad sleep last night due to the slip that his family received. A notice for every citizen of their county called New Mythian World. The deworming will begin at dusk.

Ten thousand eight hundred clock tickings (3 ancient hours) before the scariest event of the century, Hermap decided to bring his 10 children and 5 mistresses to the other side of their housetown, just below the sandy ground, maybe a mile deep. He was so nervous and his mistresses were weary, their kids were wiggling desperately, frightened.

No time to waste, the sirens on Fifty Sixth Deep had sounded already. Soldiers will knock at their door anytime and could knock anyone, anyhow. Hermap inserted his 10 wigglers on the security pockets just below his mistresses' bellies, two wigglers each. Then, he tied his 5 mistresses on his back, like a knapsack tight enough for the journey. They descended through the bathroom floor without hesitation.

They're safe now. It's dark and warm in this place but fear and danger were absent. The deworming will only last for a short time, shorter than before. They can ascend soon, back to their housetown above, maybe after a century or two.

Wango

A slippery passage beneath Mount Phoebe of Gilla Island opened to welcome a guest - an untamed, interstellar unicorn named Wango. He's one of the unsung heros of the recent conflict in Uranus.

Wango was an ally to the Phoebic Insectoid Spies who joined in their conquest of Suna, a county near Lake Bumbum. Suna is rich in precious milky mineral that was necessary for Insectoids' survival. That attack resulted into a terrorizing pandemic, an unbreakable curse that affected Sunasians' upper body parts, turning them into hydrocephalic creatures.

Inside the headquarters of the Insectoid Spies, Wango meets Qing Evib, the P.I.S.'s Queenking. He's the half-brother of Qing Trantul of Ziknakos. They talked about the reincarnation of one of the Men of Utor named Odlid, former General of the Bad Hyenas - archrival of the Insectoids.

Odlid escaped from the war and phoenixized himself for a rebirth in one of the cave systems of No-Guard-Wall. He was reborn by sticking himself on a powerful stalactite called Tilc.

No-Guard-Wall was believed to be the mother of all civilizations because of the Tilc. The cave systems there were life-giving shelters for all creatures.

Later, Qing Evib was found dead, bathe in foreign urine and intergalactic puke. The reincarnation happened 3,600 clock tickings ago.

The Leap Reckonians

There were 6 factions in the Leap Reckon county. The Marblers, the Glitterers, the Potters, the Rainbowers, the Shiniers, and the Buttoners. They're simply terrorists.

Back in the days of old, Leap Reckonians were united. They're peace-loving creatures. But because of the gold mines' closure, they became harsh to their neighbors and were engaging themselves into disputes among the people of Stripes Archipelago.

Looting, robbery and other unpleasant practices occured. And these bad traits were inherited by the new generation.

As a result of the terror that was rampant, the county of Leap Reckon was not included in the list of Southeastern allies. This county was considered as enemies' dwelling place, lair of rebels, dungeon of bandits, camp of thieves and such other common names.

Is there any hope for this county? Maybe there's nothing, nobody, and no more, for the Leap Reckonians' welfare.

To be labeled a terrorist puts anyone in a delinquent situation and in a semi-near-death experience on this half-broken Earth and even beyond this vast omniverse.

Please come and help us! Will you visit us soon?

The Heart of Tronk

Tronk left his family as an unending wildfire devoured Ynri, their beloved steady planet near the constellation Gemini. It was a hard decision for him, and wasn't a coincidence.

He traveled to the nearest Neongreen star to find luck. Maybe he could discover an oasis, where he could begin again.

Aboard an old space vehicle that his con-man grandfather gave him, Tronk was so sad, eyes teary, mind troubled. The view seen at the deck's window was so terrifying, but indeed, it was a spectacular sight.

Four darkyears later, Tronk's heart became as hard as a stone. He never ever cared about the colonies he destroyed near Uranus and the humanoid races he massacred.

There's almost nothing left in the vast omniverse save an unknown planetoid, a darkyear away from Moon Ai. Tronk felt connected to this place as he was approaching it. His newly constructed space ship, SS Ryp landed safely.

He saw some creatures a stone's throw away as he descended down the semi-rocky grassland. Rage caught his stone heart and he decided to fire his laser canon towards them, eliminating the natives in a one-hit combo.

Savage! He pulverized everything on his way...including Ryp. Until he was left alone. No connection. No more rides.

Tronk continued to circle this planetoid he named, Yrd, until he finally dried up.

The Worried Qing

For the past 69 years, no plague ever visited the Fire people of Beeshano county, near the Boring La River.

Qing Nira, their legitimate Queenking panicked as she saw a coming one while leering from one of the tower's watch holes.

A raging weather can be seen from afar. The fiery Qing summoned all her remaining battalions to be ready in doing some necessary actions. Others waged war, near the Southern Gulf together with the Sundogs.

A thousand miles away, semi-brownish clouds were present. They're like smoke mixed with manure and frozen mud.

Her greatgreatgrandfather, Qing Gof instructed to her the "Secret of Combatting a Plague" when she was just a young girl.

Qing Nira's reddish long hair raised as she shouted her commands to her soldiers to prepare the catapults.

Asphaltic brimstones will be fired directly to the center of the upcoming plague to ensure its destruction, for it's a life-threatening hazard. They must act immediately to save her Qingdom.

Bangs and booms followed. Gargantuan balls of burning rocks hit the said weather disturbance.

It's almost a year after those deadly blasts and Qing Nira still awaits the return of her million warwagers. She was so worried.

Swap

Hanct never cared about his personal skills and ability. He came from the cursed family of magicians.

He left his powers wherever he wanted. Telepathy in the classroom. Invisibility in the toilet. Necromancy at the park, just beside the broken see-saw. Others forgotten elsewhere.

Only one power was left inside his being - the Power of Cure.

One day, he saw a bleeding Unicorn with a unique horn. It was beaten by a Golemtroll last night as it passed by the burning bridge, at the eastern side of Boring La River.

Hanct don't wanted to heal it but as he touched it's unique horn, the blood hastily stopped. The silvery liquid from the Unicorn's head disappeared in an instant.

Hanct was so disappointed of his remaining power so he suggested to the unicorn that he wanted a swap.

Something from the fantastic horse in exchange to his magic.

The unicorn agreed. Hanct gave his curing ability to this beast. And then, the horny horse galloped until its unique horn was detached from its head. It's now ready to be given to Hanct.

As the poor Hanct accepted it, he slipped. Sadly, he cannot heal himself anymore.

Tod

Tod the Toadfowl was laughing at his older brother for he was missing a limb.

Everyone in the small Frughian swamp knew the Truth that this phenomenon was normal. But Tod annoyed his brother continuously and also all the Toadfowls that went through this evolutionary stage.

He's always bullied when he's alone because the other Toadfowls were actually angry due to his ridiculousness. But some of them just don't mind Tod, for they respected his father, the legitimate leader of their tribe.

Tod was born last week and he's only a wee swimmer with a very beautiful tail, blackish and shimmering

1,209,600 clock tickings later, two limbs grew on his chubby and slimy body. Tod knew that it's normal.

But after a month, Tod's other (expected) two limbs were still missing. They never appeared. What an abnormal Toadfowl!

The Igloo Tragedy

Cold was the night as the dimlight from an igloo nearby lit the background.

A hedgehog walking on the forest decided to pass by the icy area, curious of the brightness coming from the Icescream moose's shelter.

Icescream moose were very hi-tech but superstitious animals. They loved everything about science and alchemy. The forbidden wisdom of the old has a great importance.

Regarding the hedgehog, he was a poor no-name fauna that was interested about bright and shiny things just like his distant cousins - the Leap Reckonians.

The freezing breeze hit the fauna's behind as he skillfully skidded his way to the igloo.

As he approached it nearer and nearer, he could hear some splashes and squirts from the inside.

The hedgehog tried to peek through the window but all of a sudden he was freezing unto death. Some excessed butane mixed with liquified oxygen was thrown through that small vent.

Where's Mr. Gameflock?

Our school was full of mischievous Stew Dents, sons and daughters of Tooth Fairies that squatted for a long time in the suburbs of Ngi Pin City.

Mr. Gameflock was the newly assigned principal and he's in-charged of the Guidance Dept. of this institution too.

One day, he saw a young Stew Dent on graffiti mode by the sidewall of the school. He pulled over his Chewbrewlette and tried to catch the running infidel. Vandalism was a major offense.

Luckily, Principal Gameflock never ever caught anyone since the day he started teaching. That silly Stew Dent escaped. Sadly, Mr. Gameflock did not recognize the offender's face.

He was very angry that's why he recharged a spared Chewbrewlette battery, and then connected it onto the walls of the campus, hoping to stop vandalism.

That was Saturday morning, the Tooth Fairy community circled around a scene. A fat nincompoop was decomposing at the backside wall of the old school. By looking at it, this guy suffered from the highest degree of burning.

The First Refugees

A spark from the sky can be seen from the mouth of this cave where we lived for the past thousand years.

A strange curve line appeared in a sudden, hit the Foi Tree where we're picking our daily need of protein. The fruits ignited as a line of light touched the Foi's broadness.

I was so shocked of this peculiar sighting but also thrilled and excited about the ignition that occured.

I braced myself in the sprouting stalagmite as a shockwave passed our dwelling. My wife was awakened by its bang, crawled unto me and shared her shivers as the quake disappeared little by little.

I closed my eyes, begged the deities for protection. I was worried not for my being but for my wife and 35 children.

It's almost dawn, my fear subsided. We're safe. Yes, we were safe now.

About the Author

W. J. Manares

W. J. Manares a. k. a. Willer Jun Araneta Manares is a one-of-a-kind persona in the literary scene of Aklan - the oldest province in the Philippines. He came out from his mother's birth canal on the 1st day of June, year 1985.

He came from a prominent Hispanic family. A legitimate member of Familia Araneta (Araneta Family) in the Philippines, included in its 7th generation, to be exact.

He's the Philippine Brand Ambassador of Noel Lorenz House of Fiction, India and a member of The Aklan Literati (AkLit).

A semi-religious fellow who loves everything erotic and sci-fi. A volunteer teacher with a philanthropic heart. And a freelance musical coach if needed.

A lesser-known writer and worldbuilder who was influenced by the Superstar, Piers Anthony especially by his books, But What of Earth? Bio of an Ogre, and Ogre, Ogre. He built the worlds of Stripes Archipelago and Nation of Tseicurdia.

His children's story, "Ro Mga Busoe Ni Noel" got the consolation prize in the Aklanon category of Aliwanag, a story writing contest by Aklat Alamid & Kasingkasing Press.

He authored seven self-published books: Archipelago Astray, Isa Sa Ilang Paraan, Pilang Ka Sugid-sugid sa Bibi it Akean, Ang Bulbul atbp., Sa Itim Na Butas Ako'y Dumausdos 6.9, HAY and Mabilis na Pagyaman.

His High Fantasy story, Dormancy Breakage, was included in the NLHF and Country Girrls anthology, Risqué. His poem, Just Like A Rabbit, was also included in Cooch Behar's Year of the Rabbit Anthology. His works were also included in Cooch Behar Anthology Volume 5 and Anthology of Poets, Short Stories and Journey, edited by Sourav Sarkar. Recently, his poem, WATER'S PROOFS was one of the inclusions in Save Water Anthology of the same editor. These books are available on Amazon.

He received the Charles Bukowski Poetry Award recently for his poesy and international involvement for the propagation of poetic works.

His "BetLog: Titiliang Tala, Tatalaang Tula" and "Tanaga, Diyona... Dalit? Mga Tulang May Pusong Pinoy (with English translation)" are published by Ukiyoto Publishing.

He also started his own literary magazine, Wellerism, to cater the exposure of freelance writers locally and some others too.

He's also a songwriter and loves to strum the guitar and sing. He loves the music of Rammstein, Red Hot Chili Peppers, Green Day, Eagle-Eye Cherry and Toad the Wet Sprocket. He also wrote religious songs before.

When not writing, he's in his own library, reading and stacking his collection of books up on the shelves again and again.

He loves the taste of cinnamon sometimes. He enjoys living his peculiar life near the gateway to the paradise island of Boracay.

www.ingramcontent.com/pod-product-compliance
Lightning Source LLC
LaVergne TN
LVHW041642070526
838199LV00053B/3516

* 9 7 8 9 3 6 0 1 6 7 3 7 0 *